Why Was Six Afraid of Seven? by Es Kay Johns

For information regarding permission, write to eskayjohns@gmail.com

Published by: Es Kay Johns Publishing
Text and Illustration by: Es Kay Johns
Library of Congress Control Number: 2016911750
ISBN: 978-0-9978217-1-0

10 9 8 7 6 5 4 3 2 1

1. Children's book 2. Children's humor

First Edition

Thank you for your support of "Why was Six Afraid of Seven?"
It is my desire to inspire young readers to discover the joy and
imagination that comes with reading and mathematics.

Please help me reach a larger audience by spreading this series and
its messages to children all around the world.

If you like this story and would like to view others,
please visit www.eskayjohns.com for more readings such as,
"What Did Zero Say to Eight?"

WHY WAS SIX AFRAID OF SEVEN?

Written and Illustrated by
Es Kay Johns

Number Chronicles

Six sat down at his desk
wanting to start his homework,
but he couldn't.
He was just so tired from
soccer practice.

Name: ____
1+1 = ____
4+3 = ____
7+9 = ____
8+0 = ____

Doing Math homework made
Six feel slow like a slug and slightly
sleepy. But he yawned and started
anyway.

"One plus one equals two. Four plus three equals...it equals..."

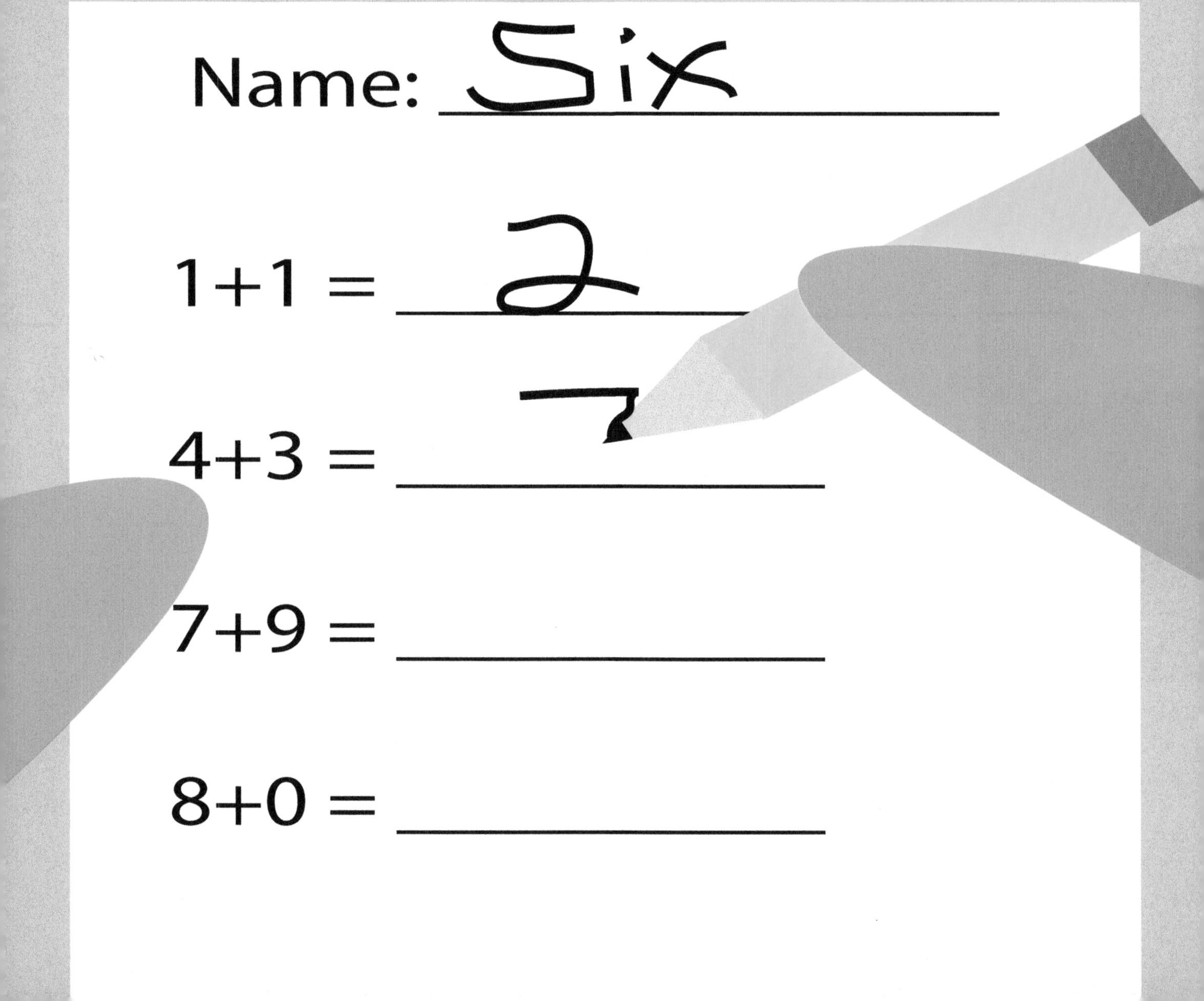

Name: Six

$1+1 =$ 2

$4+3 =$ 7

$7+9 =$ _____

$8+0 =$ _____

Six's eyes closed and
he started to snore.

"Four goals!" Six screamed after scoring against Seven in soccer.
He ran to the sideline where Nine was sitting.

He sat on the bench and gave Nine a high-five.
"That was a great kick you did, Six!" said Nine.

**Turning towards Seven, Nine shouted,
"Seven, you stink!"**

Seven was embarrassed and mad that Nine
was being mean to him!

Instead of letting Nine know that his feelings were hurt,
he ran over to the bench and ate him!

Seven ate Nine!

Six was shocked!
He looked at Seven and saw that he was still mad.

He was afraid that Seven would eat him next,
so he ran across the soccer field!

He turned and yelled "Stop!"

But Seven
ate him too!

Seven rubbed his belly and said, "They won't mess with me anymore!"

Six woke up from his nightmare!

Realizing that he did not finish his homework, he carefully solved the rest of the problems.

Name: Six

1+1= 2
4+3= 7
7+9= 16
8+0= 8

The next day at soccer practice,
Six shared his bad dream with some of his teammates.
"Seven ate Nine?!" Zero gasped.

"Yes, Seven ate Nine. I was so afraid,"
Six responded.

Zero and Eight continued to practice soccer while
Six, Seven, and Nine sat on the bench to talk.

"I'd never eat Nine! I would have told him that his comments
upset and embarrassed me," said Seven.

Nine replied, "And I would have apologized for hurting Seven's feelings.
We shouldn't bully others."

Six was happy that it was just a dream.
He knows that bullying is wrong and there are better ways to
handle embarrassing situations.

So, why was Six afraid of Seven?
Because...

I'd like to thank Kickstarter and all of the backers of

Why Was Six Afraid of Seven?

This book would not exist without all of you.

I'd like to give the following special thanks to:

Giancarlo
Thank you for pushing me to keep chasing my dreams.
You stood by me 100% of the time and kept me moving forward.
Your love and encouragement will always keep me going.

Geana
Thank you for your creative mind that
helped me shape things when I could not.

Moyo
Thank you for reviewing/editing the story when it was just starting out.

Freddy
Thank you for your dedicated support and amazing technical skills.
Our web presence makes all the difference.

Shae, Nicole, and Noon
My brother and his beautiful family constantly
reviewed, edited, and worked with me to get the story and
its images to where it needed to be. I'm very thankful for all of their expertise.